Boot Camp

"Training Teachers for Service"

by Rocheroyl Lowery

Copyright © 2002 by Rocheroyl Lowery

Boot Camp
by Rocheroyl Lowery

Printed in the United States of America

Library of Congress Control Number: 2002107767
ISBN 1-591601-43-6

All rights reserved. No part of this publication may be reproduced or transmitted in any form or by any means without written permission of the author.

**Salah Ministries
P.O. Box 1382
Calumet City, IL. 60409**
E-mail: salahministries@aol.com

Unless otherwise indicated, Bible quotations are taken from the King James Version of the Bible.

Note: The name satan and related names are not capitalized. We choose not to acknowledge him, even to the point of violating grammatical rules.

Xulon Press
11350 Random Hills Road, Suite 800
Fairfax, VA 22030
(703) 279-6511
XulonPress.com

To order additional copies, call 1-866-909-BOOK (2665).

Book cover design by MJB Graphics
Edited by Josephine Sharif

Dedication

I want to dedicate this book first and foremost to my Lord and Savior Jesus Christ, to my great and long standing teacher *Holy Spirit*, and to my faithful Father, The Almighty God, Jehovah-Elohim.

To my mother and aunt, Ernestine and Anniestine, who raised me with absolutely nothing but unconditional love: I thank you both from the bottom of my heart.

To my pastor at Valley Kingdom Ministries International and friend who has lead me through some of my most difficult *learning* years, my covering, Apostle H. Daniel Wilson and his Proverb's 31 woman, my example, Pastor Beverly L. Wilson

Finally, to my anointed son Stuart, who has shared me with thousands and never once openly complained about having a ministering Mom: Thanks for "Salah;" I love you beyond measure.

Words of Thanks

To my teachers, the late Pastor Theodore H. McFarland,Sr., the late Deacon Andrew Hyman, Sr., Pastor Elaine L. Graham and Elder Linda J. Smith; Thank you for being visionaries in my life and for believing in me and the God who created me.

To Josephine S. I don't know what I would have done without you.

And to all of the great teachers, preachers and students who have gone through my classroom doors and, by the grace of God, have picked up a little something on the way: I continue to speak blessings into your life.

About the Book

The United States of America armed forces have a valid requirement to have a relatively large number of professional armed men and women in place at all times, prepared to fight for our great country on a moment's notice. On September 10, 2001, during my bible study time God gave me a revelation about war; and on September 11, 2001, there was a terrorist attack on America. I believe that our armed forces have been blessed, in that we have always stood in a pretty good position from a security stand point. However, September 11, 2001, found us unprepared. The terrorist's commandeered commercial aircraft on a kamikaze mission crashing into the Twin Towers of the World Trade Center in New York and the Pentagon in Washington, D.C. Thousands of people were injured and killed. Damage was done to individuals, families, properties and, businesses. Words cannot begin to express the heart felt sorrow and mental anguish experienced by billions throughout the United States and all over the world. To this day, we still do not realize the full impact. Let us continue to pray for our nation.

Now that the United States is on full military alert, what about the Church, the Christian family, the spiritual army of God? What kind of position are we in? Can we declare war on the kingdom of darkness without backing down? Are we prepared for the attacks of the enemy? Wake up and smell the spiritual coffee, there is an attack assignment with your name on it and satan is not going to back down. My spiritual general, Apostle H. Daniel Wilson often says something to this effect: Either you're in a battle, coming out of one or one is headed in your direction. How are you going to handle it?

I ask, are the ascension-gifted teachers of God ready? Are we prepared as children of God, to prepare others? I once thought this was such an unusual generation, but the closer I look, the more I see (backed up by the Word of God), that people are pretty much the same. Yes, people want God or a form of God but not according to knowledge. This world is filled with people who know of God and want God somewhere in their life, but according to **their terms**. There's another group that says, I just want the truth, I want the Word of God alive in my life so give it to me straight, don't sugar it up, don't water it down. Teach me that I may know Him, and that I may tell others. This generation of teachers must be equipped to tell the Gospel truth. The purpose of this book is to prepare this "new jack", generation of teachers. The Gospel has to stay the same, but the methods in which we teach it, preach it and share it must change with each new generation.

For years I've searched for information that would be helpful in training teachers for service. Some literature seemed to offer lots of information, but little application and real experience. I've found as a Christian teacher we need both, data (information) and application (experience). The more I sought information, the more questions evolved. Questions like; What are the tools to help me in the thinking process? Who's helping the Christian teacher? Where can I get the hands on "application" training?

As Christians we've been taught to trust and rely upon Holy Spirit as our teacher, our illuminator and our inspiration. I also believe Christian teachers need something tangible, in our hands, something that could be used as a reference over and over again to continuously prepare us for greater works and encourage us. Clearly we need the Word of God, the Holy Bible, and this explains my assignment.

In December 1998 I received the revelation of this assignment and began to write the vision down. Little did I know that it would develop into this book. The same question that started my writing adventure, I pose to you: Are *you* willing to go back to **boot camp** and revisit your training ground?

For some teachers this may be a brand new experience. For others, it means bringing out the old army gear- the spiritual uniform, hat and boots- and learning new drills and strategies. Do you have the discipline and stamina it takes to go back to a boot camp? Boot camp requires that you develop a detailed schedule of regiment training and study. We must remain true to our God and to our duty, being careful to teach (not our version of the truth) but the untainted, unspoiled "straight up" truth.

After more than twenty-five blessed years of ministering in the area of Christian Education, I have been released to share some of the nuggets and truths that God has given me. Look at it this way, I'm just following the orders of my Chief Commander (Holy Spirit) who instructed me to write it down:

Habakkuk 2:2 Write the vision, and make it plain upon tables, that he may run that readeth it.

Therefore, within these pages, it is my prayer that this book will minister to all the saints of God, especially new teachers, but also to the experienced teachers who have been on the "battle field" of teaching for the Lord for years.

In this book you will go through a "boot camp" training. "***Boot Camp***," is a back to basic, down to earth, simplistic teaching course for both new and mature teachers. This book is serious about teacher preparation, but somewhat humorous and refreshing. You'll gain insight and new ideas. It is also ***our*** desire that you learn how to develop and begin a "hands on" Boot Camp **Teachers Training Program** within your Church, ministry or outreach.

We'll cover some areas you have probably visited or studied before, but don't despair- Our God has a way of breathing on it all over again and blessing it so that it becomes fresh. If you are a teacher, I

About the Book

encourage you to be very serious about your continued preparation. If you're not sure and looking for direction, I pray this book will shed light on your concealed areas of expertise and give you insight. This is not just a book that's good for your collection, but one that will encourage you and re-energized you for continued service. No matter what your boot size (apostles, prophets, evangelists, pastors, teachers or laymen boots), your skill level or experience, you'll fit in well, in **Boot Camp.**

Contents

Foreword by Apostle H. Daniel Wilson xvii

Chapter I—New Recruits and Re-enlisters 18

Chapter II—Basic Training. 35

Chapter III—R & R: Rank and Responsibility . . 49

Chapter IV—Know Your Weapons 65

Chapter V—Strategies (Part I) 83

Chapter VI—Strategies (Part II). 95

Foreword

If there is one thing that I have clearly seen in my twenty-three years of ministry and nineteen years of pastoring, it is the lack of knowledge of the people of God concerning spiritual warfare. We sing "I'm a soldier in the army of the Lord", and we read that the weapons of our warfare are not carnal but mighty to the pulling down of strongholds. However so many saints are totally unprepared to fight the spiritual war against our spiritual enemy satan, that we need training for warring in the spirit. This is why I am ecstatic and excited about the content of this book ***Boot Camp: Preparing Teachers for Service***, by Elder Rocheroyl Lowery.

In the ten years that Elder Lowery has served in our ministry, I have observed her in several key areas, including Sunday School Superintendent, Director of Christian Education and now as the Pastor of Church Operations of Valley Kingdom

Ministries International.

Elder Lowery is a Bible student as well as teacher of the Word of God, and she does both with intensity, intelligence and excellence.

This book will become one of the premier instruction agents to prepare teachers, to prepare Christian soldiers for war. The United States without question has the greatest military in the history of the world. And the primary reason is that before we send our soldiers **out** to fight we bring them **in** to boot camp for training.

Elder Lowery, as the master drill instructor, has been gifted by God to prepare our spiritual drill sergeants with tools and training to equip our spiritual recruits, *not only for warring war, but tools for winning this war.* Get ready to be blessed, challenged and changed as you enter into **Boot Camp**, for this book will strengthen your faith and fortify you to say about this spiritual war, **"I'm in it, and I've been trained to win it."**

In Him,

Apostle H. Daniel Wilson, Senior Pastor
Valley Kingdom Ministries International

Chapter I

New Recruits and Re-enlisters

[Re-cruit]- New enlisted personnel
[Re-in-listed]- To reenter or continue

Recruits learn to be soldiers during boot camp. Normally in the U.S. Army the training lasts about eight weeks. We're going to go as long as it takes. Holy Spirit has given me the duty of being your temporary drill sergeant, however, you must spend one-on-one time with Him for personal instructions.

Making a decision to enlist in this spiritual military service is not one that should be taken lightly. It can't be made out of indecisiveness or boredom. On the contrary, this decision is so extremely important, it's only one that can be made after serious consideration and prayer. This is a real battle. A battle against knowing and not knowing. The enemy has set up road blocks to stop you from studying and coming to know the truth in the Word of God. My assignment is to point out the traps, reveal the truth and get you on the right track. Maybe you're not a teacher, but you need the tools of the trade to develop a good study habit, welcome. This army is not one of guns and physical weapons but a spiritual war against, believe it or not, knowledge and ignorance. The Bible says we are destroyed for lack of knowledge.

Hos 4:6 My people are destroyed for lack of knowledge:

In addition we must be careful not to reject knowledge. **... because thou hast rejected knowledge, I will also reject thee, that thou shalt be no priest to me: seeing thou hast forgotten the law of thy God, I will also forget thy children.**

Re-enlisting is recommitment, rededication to serve and service again. The difference in the Christian army and the U.S. Army is that God takes you back even if you were AWOL (absent without leave). In fact His Word tells us He (God) is married to the backslider (Jeremiah 3:14).

Several years ago in a little store front church on the west side of Chicago, where Bible study sometimes consisted of three or four people (one of them being the pastor), God birthed a love in me for the reading and studying of His Holy Word. Pastor taught me at an early age to *study*, search the scriptures out, get the truth, allow Holy Spirit to teach you and come to know the truth for yourself.

2 Timothy 2:15 Study to shew thyself approved unto God, a workman that needeth not to be

ashamed, rightly dividing the word of truth.

He said we must study the Word of God to show ourselves approved unto God. In other words, don't shame Him when we speak of Him or His Word. He taught me to meditate on His Word day and night, even as Joshua had been instructed. Joshua 1:8 **thou shalt meditate therein day and night, that thou mayest observe to do according to all that is written therein:** My pastor at the time explained this is a key to being prosperous and having good success, by being obedient to the Word of God. Joshua 1:8 goes on to say: **for then thou shalt make thy way prosperous, and then thou shalt have good success.** How much study time should you put in? Let me ask you how successful do you want to be?

We should never rely on the words of someone else to be our road map, when we can *study the road map for ourselv*es.

I'll never forget the months of Bible study spent on two or three verses from the Bible. Back then, as a child both spiritually and physically, I had no idea of the direction that God was taking me, nor of the "boots" he wanted me to wear, but, one thing was for sure, I knew I loved the Lord, and I wanted to know more about Him. What I didn't realize was, I was being drawn closer to Him and he was drawing closer to me.

James 4:8 Draw nigh to God, and he will draw nigh to you.

He was actually enlisting me into His army. Jesus was developing a relationship with me that I might know Him.

Philippians 3:10 That I may know him, and the power of his resurrection, and the fellowship of his sufferings...

Yes, I wanted to know Him, but I didn't know what it took to *really* get to know Him. Let's first get an understanding of what is needed or necessary when enlisting into an army rather than being drafted.

Draft or Enlist

Anyone interested in joining the U.S. Armed Forces knows full well that you don't get in by sitting on the couch. You've got to get up, go to your recruiting office and enlist or sign on the dotted line. But above all, you must *want* to serve your country. As it is with your Savior, you must *want* to serve Him. Service or serving has nothing to do with your education, what you look like, your talents or abilities. But rather your commitment and a real desire to serve. I remember back in the 1970s there was something called the draft. The purpose of the draft was to create and maintain an overflow of physically fit men and women to be prepared to go to battle if needed, to defend our great country the U.S.A. This draft process sent you whether you wanted to go or not. Here's where we differ from the U.S. army. You've got to be a *willing* vessel.

As with any army, there's is an recruitment process. We could stop and make a big deal out of whether you enlisted or were drafted. With many of us being teachers we would debate back and for for a long time. But let's settle it by going to the manual, the Bible. God says He chose you, you were drafted.

John 15:16 Ye have not chosen me, but I have chosen you, and ordained you.

God has spoken. It is settled. If you're reading this book you're either sure of your assignment or you're trying to find out what God wants you to do. He wants you to be fruitful! Keep reading!

John 15:16 continues, **ye should go and bring forth fruit, and that your fruit should remain** To bring forth fruit means to be productive. When God has chosen you to work, your fruit should be evident. If you're in the same spiritual position that you've been in for the past twenty years, where's your fruit? Same storefront church (I have nothing against storefront churches, I was raised in a good one.) same running toilet, same falling wall paper, same peeling paint.... Where's your fruit? Check out the fruit. God never told you to *create* the fruit; you are to preserve it, and take care of it and allow it to multiply. In fact, God has given you everything you need to keep the multiplication going. Look at a few more scriptures:

Genesis 1:22 **And God blessed them, saying, Be fruitful, and *multiply*, and fill the waters in the seas, and let fowl *multiply* in the earth**.

Genesis 1:28-29 **And God blessed them, and God said unto them, Be fruitful, and *multiply*, and replenish the earth, and subdue it: and have dominion over the fish of the sea, and over the fowl of the air, and over every living thing that** moveth upon the earth. **And God said, Behold, I have given you every herb bearing seed, which is upon the face of all the earth, and every tree, in the which** *is* **the fruit of a tree yielding seed; to you it shall be for meat.**

He even instructed Noah to be fruitful but he was never asked to create it.

Genesis 8:17 **Bring forth with thee every living thing that is with thee, of all flesh, both of fowl, and of cattle, and of every creeping thing that creepeth upon the earth; that they may breed abundantly in the earth, and be fruitful, and** *multiply* **upon the earth.**

The word multiply in the Hebrew translation is *rabah* (raw-baw), it means to increase, bring in abundance, be in authority, enlarge, excel, nourish, exceed and grow.

To Be Chosen

Even though you were chosen, what was your answer? Can you say your answer was yes? Or are you just going along for the ride? Yes, you were chosen, but we serve a God of liberty, who is not going to push His way in or force you to make a decision. He lays the evidence before you, and you can take if from there!

Matthew 22:14 For many are called, but few are chosen.

It's clear that everyone from the least to the greatest has been called unto salvation. (Salvation, being delivered from the power and the penalty of sin over your life by repenting of your sins and accepting Jesus Christ as your Lord and Savior.) Now let's look at the "few are chosen." I may need to go back down memory lane for this one. Back in my high school days, to be chosen meant, to be picked, going steady, when you were chosen you were *spoken for*. In the Greek this chosen means pretty much the same: to be selected, chosen out from among, very highly, ask, call, put forth.

2 Peter 3:9 The Lord is not slack concerning his promise, as some men count slackness; but is long-suffering to us-ward, not *willing that any should perish, but that all should come to repentance.*

You were chosen unto salvation.

If you enlisted, that means you signed up because it is something you wanted to do. We must know beyond the shadow of a doubt that God has called you unto and into this great ministry. Most days you'll want to teach, but some days you'll say, "I just want to rest." And I found out God will allow you to rest in Him, but not on the job. Don't get me wrong, God wants you to have a balanced life. Just don't get lazy or sloth.

Psalm 37:7 Rest in the Lord

Genesis 2:2-3 And on the seventh day God ended his work which he had made; and he rested on the seventh day from all his work which he had made. And God blessed the seventh day, and sanctified it: because that in it he had rested from all his work which God created and made.

God rested after the work of creation. It's time to work now, you've rested long enough.

As Apostle H. Daniel Wilson would say, it's time to take your thin skin off, because I'm about to make a few statements that some may not like, but many need to hear anyway.

Believe it or not, some teachers stand before God and the assembly of His people teaching because they have a desire to teach, some because they desire to be seen or like the sound of their voice, some because they like control, leadership position, and for many other reasons. Understand this, there are consequences that come with being a teacher of the Gospel of Jesus Christ.

James 3:1 My breathren, be not many masters (teachers) knowing that we shall receive the greater condemnation.

In other words, everybody is not a teacher; in fact, teachers will be judged more strictly than others. You better know for yourself, that each person must give an account *for himself*. Don't teach because it makes you look or feel good; this is serious business- it's a calling- you were selected by God Himself to fulfill this assignment.

Who Contacted You?

In the U.S. military, if you've been drafted by the government, they contacted you. When God drafted (ordained you, called you out, summoned you, sanctified you, set you aside) you to this work, you still had a choice to accept the assignment or reject it. Please hear me: If you have been called to minister in this area and you try to do anything else, it may look nice, but it's not going to prosper, its not going to flourish. I hear you out there: But what if it changes the lives of thousands? Great, but was that what God told you to do? *I believe, it will burn up as dry leaves before God as you stand before him to obtain your rewards, because it was not your assignment.*

If God gave you an assignment, when you proceed, it will flourish like the palm tree and shall grow like a cedar in Lebanon in other words big time!

Psalm 92:12-13 The righteous shall flourish like the palm tree: he shall grow like a cedar in Lebanon. Those that be planted in the house of the LORD shall flourish in the courts of our God.

So, if you thought you were teaching because it's just something you like to do, think again! Teaching is a intricate part of the ascension gift. When Jesus ascended He gave gifts to the body.

Eph 4:11-12 And he gave some, apostles; and some, prophets; and some, evangelists; and some, pastors and teachers; For the perfecting of the saints, for the work of the ministry for the edifying of the body of Christ.

Many people have referred to the ascension gifts as the "Five fold ministry," from here on throughout this book we will refer to them as the ascension gifts.

The Baby Finger

Speaking of the ascension gifts, I've got to share a story with you that my Christian sister Minister Michele Aikens told me. One day she was speaking with one of her relatives who tried to convince her that because teaching is listed as the last of the ascension gifts, it is obviously the least important. He began to count off each area of the ascension gifts, quoting the scripture and using his fingers to identify each ministry. Her relative said, "And he gave some, apostles (the thumb); and some, prophets (the pointer finder); and some, evangelists (the middle finder); and some, pastors (the ring finder); and teachers (the little baby finger);" then he stuck his little finger in his ear and proceeded to clean his ear out thus demonstrating how insignificant that little finger was. Initially, I was offended, Michele and I both being educators, we became concerned, then angry, then frustrated (*Yep*, we're human). Why was he belittling teaching? Why was teaching considered the least important? But, thanks be unto God he "caught us," and Holy Spirit began to minister to us and turn that thing around. We both got the revelation (Thank You Jesus!) that it is the little finger that cleans the ear, it's the little finger that gets into the inner ear, no other finger can do that. Today I realize it's not how we look, how important it looks or doesn't look ,but what matters most is whether it is for God's glory.

Isaiah 55:8-9 For my thoughts *are* not your thoughts, neither *are* your ways my ways, saith

the LORD. 9 For *as* **the heavens are higher than the earth, so are my ways higher than your ways, and my thoughts than your thoughts.**

That same little "insignificant" baby finger, got deep enough into his hearing sensory to clean it up, relieve the annoying itch and bring comfort all at the same time with just a little tug or shake. Thank You Jesus for that little finger, it sure is needed as a part of this great body.

Proof of Thy Ministry

Let's look at enlisting. If you enlist, you make a contractual agreement with the army, where you choose to serve in the military. The army did not select you but you chose to participate in it on your own. Saints of God, be sure of your calling. Join the army of the Lord- not because you're looking for something to do, because you like the uniform, because you like the shining badges and awards- but join because you realize this is the ministry and work that the LORD has called you unto, allowed you to join, and because you realize there is a war going on.

- Not for the prestige, because the more you speak the truth, it appears the more folks won't like you.
- Don't look for recognition, look for God's righteousness.
- Don't look for a pat on the back, look for the praises that will go unto the Father.

Once you personally understand your calling (it's a, *personal* thing ,you see), then you can go forth.

2 Timothy 4:3 reminds us that the time is coming (I believe it is here right now) when people won't want to listen to good teaching. Instead they will want to hear teachers who will say what they want to hear, teachers who will please them by telling them what their itching ears want to hear. They will turn from the truth and eagerly listen to senseless stories. But you must stay calm and be willing to teach. You must work hard to tell the Good News (Gospel) and to do your job well in other words **"make full proof of thy ministry". (2 Timothy 4:5)**

What you'll notice about your assignment, (and others will notice it in you) in time: You'll have a labor of love for teaching and you'll develop a militant spirit. I like to call it *passion*.

A Love Thang

To love to teach and study the Word is not enough, you've got to love the Word of God, and the God of the Word so much until you become obedient to what He says. As a teacher I found it was possible to love the Word,

love to study,
love the diggin',
love the research,
love the teaching,
love the preparation for teaching,

love the anointing,
but not love the Lord enough to be obedient. **Ouch!**

Teachers must be extremely watchful and careful in this area. Why? I'm glad you asked. Because we're upfront and center and can like or even *love* to hear ourselves teach, preach and proclaim the Good News! God wants us to love **Him**. We've got to know it's a combination of study and obedience. I see the raised eyebrows. You don't have to believe me, let's go to God's Word.

John 14:15 If ye love me, keep my commandments. John 14:23 Jesus answered and said unto him, If a man love me, he will keep my words: and my Father will love him, and we will come unto him, and make our abode with him.

It's about LOVE, if you love Him.

John 15:10 *If ye keep my commandments, ye shall abide in my love*; **even as I have kept my Father's commandments, and** *abide in his love*.

Recognize that God is laying foundational truths in you and Holy Ghost is teaching us to love Him and His Word. What we must do is show this love in our sharing the wonderful Word of God through teaching. We must be walking it, talking it, breathing it, living it, every day. It's not something you can pretend to love, because let's face it, everybody knows when it's just an *act-*, Holy Ghost discernment (not carnal thinking) will tell you that. Let me just throw in the difference between judgment and discernment. *Judgment* is when you look at others and see their faults; *discernment* is when you first look at your self and see how you line up with the Word of God.

Your love and compassion for people will be on automatic. Your teaching will *always* be on automatic. You won't stop to think, *Should I teach now?* It's automatic. Real "called" teachers will know what I'm talking about; no matter where you are, you find yourself teaching. In the grocery store teaching, in the home teaching, at the bus stop teaching, on the job, teaching. As with any calling or vocation, you've got to walk worthy in that area.

Ephesians 4:1 I therefore, the prisoner of the Lord, beseech you that ye walk worthy of the vocation wherewith ye are called.

Stand up straight, recruit! And walk!

Work Page 1

Recruit: Take a few moments to reflect on your assignment as a teacher. When you received your assignment, how was your assignment confirmed? Can you recall how you began to hunger and thirst after righteousness and the knowledge of God? Simply use the space below to document your past or present experiences, to begin understanding the importance of your assignment. **Drop and give Him 20! Give 10 reasons you must share this great Gospel and 10 reasons to Praise God.**

_____

_____

_____

_____

1.

2.

3.

4.

5.

6.

7.

8.

9.

10.

11.

12.

13.

14.

15.

16.

17.

18.

19.

20.

CHAPTER II

Basic Training

As I mentioned earlier, basic training generally lasts about eight weeks. It prepares an individual to be in top physical shape for battle, if required. Remember basic training is physically demanding, wimps don't make it through basic training they give up, pack there bags and go home- that's not for you.

If you report for duty in good physical shape the demand on your body (physical and spiritual) is less strenuous; however, if you report in poor shape because you have not exercised, because you have not eaten properly, or because you have not obtained proper rest, it becomes an extremely hard task.

Let's look at it using the same data from a spiritual perspective. If you have not gotten proper exercise (picked up your Bible and read it, studied it, memorized scriptures or even meditated on it), if you have not eaten properly (you have not chewed on the

Word, nor fasted when God instructed you to do so), if you have not gotten proper rest (this was hard for me. God wants His children, including teachers, to have a balanced life, and that also means getting proper rest and relaxation- If you have not done any of the above, you will be out of shape and need a healthier spiritual regiment.

Therefore, as you report for duty or re-enlist please consider what kind of shape you're in-

Let's not lose any sleep over where you are now, but let's start look at where you're going! The Apostle Paul told us:

Philippians 3:13 Brethren, I count not myself to have apprehended: but *this* one thing I do, forgetting those things which are behind, and reaching forth unto those things which are before.

If you're reporting in poor shape it could be because you have not yielded to the prompting of Holy Ghost or you have not kept your spirit in proper spiritual shape. Perhaps you have not read your Bible, nor studied like you should: maybe you have not sat under any consistent teaching to obtain, knowledge; maybe your diet is not balance with prayer, praise, and private worship. Don't despair, suck it up and let's get in shape!

Fatigues

One of the first things a recruit does when entering the military is obtain his uniform or fatigues. The clothing is important because it helps you to identify,

every day, *who* you are serving. You take off the old "street clothes" and put on the new.

Isaiah 61:3 ...beauty for ashes, the oil of joy for mourning, the garment of praise for the spirit of heaviness;

Get rid of the stale thinking and a messed up mind set. In a uniform you're dressed from head to toe. Get up, take the ashes off your face and oil yourself down with the oil of joy. No more negative "woe is me" mentality, the Bible tells us to take "the garment of praise for the spirit of heaviness." God wants us to glorify him in all that we do, even in what we wear and in our appearance. This appearance is not just physical but mental.

Romans 12:2 And be not conformed to this world but be ye transformed by the renewing of your mind that ye may prove what *is that good*, and acceptable, and perfect, will of God.

A renewed mind is a refreshed mind- A well dressed mind, a Kingdom mind.

What about your physical appearance? Is it appealing to the Lord? Can someone look at you and say, Good Lord, I know that person is blessed! Not because of the diamonds on your fingers, or the Ralph Lauren or Hugo Boss designer fashions you wear, but let it be because of your persona, your character and your walk with the Lord. Because of your love, honesty, integrity, and humble spirit and other Godly attire, you should look like Christ and you should look like you're blessed all the time!

Army Gear

In addition, when we dress we should also be geared up for battle. **Ephesians 6:11, 13-18 Put on the whole armour of God, that ye may be able to stand against the wiles of the devil... Wherefore take unto you the whole armour of God, that ye may be able to withstand in the evil day,... therefore, having your loins girt about with truth, and having on the breastplate of righteousness; And your feet shod with the preparation of the gospel of peace; Above all taking the shield of faith, ... And take the helmet of salvation, and the sword of the Spirit, which is the Word of God**:

Praying always... Seven pieces of armour. Keep in mind there are both defensive armour for protection and offensive armour for conquest. We'll address the offensive armour a little more in the chapter on *Know your weapons*. Our defensive gear protects us and should be a part of your daily uniform.

- Belt of truth
- Breastplate of righteousness
- Shoes of readiness
- Shield of Faith
- Helmet of Salvation
- Sword of the Spirit/Word of God
- Power of Prayer

Defensive Armour

I can even hear in my spirit now that we are to cover up and guard our consecrated areas. An area consecrated unto the Lord is an area that has been devoted wholly and holy unto Him. An area that has been dedicated to God and for His Glory. What areas of your physical and mental body have you consecrated to God? Have you given Him your heart? Have you given Him your feet to take you where He wants you to go? Is your assurance and faith in Him or in the things and people of this world? Have you consecrated your mind to Him and your spirit? Perhaps that's something we need to touch and agree on right now!

Father in the name of Jesus Christ we come together touching and agreeing that my new friend the reader of this book will dedicate his/her mind to Your glory. We realize that this means our way of thinking must change. We pull down the strong holds of negative thinking, lack, "that will do" attitude, that "can't do" spirit; and we take the words of "I don't see how it can happen" out of our lips and we exchange them for Your Word, "I can do all things through Christ Jesus who strengthens me". Our confidence is in You. Be glorified in this work, In Jesus' name we pray. Amen.

Belt of Truth

The purpose of the belt is to hold the other pieces

of your gear up and in place. Can you imagine a soldier going to war and his pants won't stay up, but keep falling down? Now, can you imagine a Christian that does not stand upon truth? That's just it, he can't stand on a lie. The belt of truth refers to the truthfulness found in Christians. A believer whose life is tainted with lies, deceit and craftiness eliminates the very thing we stand for. Crazy huh? When you start to lie, everything falls apart; The truth holds everything in place.

Breastplate of Righteousness

The breastplate covers the chest area, breasts, ribs and lungs, all vital organs of the body- But especially the heart.

While serving in my position as Pastor of Operations for my church, one of my responsibilities was to oversee a construction project in excess of over six million dollars. We were nearly down to the finish line and needed to close out for our opening day. Everyone was over zealous with excitement, and tension was in the air. I asked one individual question (don't even remember what the question was), but it sent that person on a wild tangent of screaming, raving and spitting hurtful words. The person slammed the telephone down in my ear and I just looked in amazement. As I recall, I could literally feel the hand of God cover my heart; I was overwhelm with such love and such peace, warmth and compassion; as I think back, it was such love. I could feel His presence IN me. I knew God had covered my heart, I felt no pain. The Rocheroyl (west side) in me wanted to be angry, I even tried to feel anger, but at that moment, I couldn't even tell what anger felt like. Wow, that blew my mind! I immediately called a friend and told her what happen, giving thanks to God for what He had done. His hand/breastplate protected me from the harsh blows, catching the fiery darts in His hand. You need your breastplate in this field of battle.

Shoes of Readiness

Our feet must be ready to go and share the Gospel whenever and wherever He sends us. Have you ever stubbed your toe? I don't know about you but if I stub my toe, you will see me hop on one foot, spin around and limp to a seat and immediately rub my toe. (It's quite a sight) But these shoes of readiness protect my feet against the traps and snares of the devil, sharp sticks of self-righteousness and the hard rocks or religion. These shoes help me to march in the right direction and in peace.

Shield of Faith

The shield of faith, above all, emphasis on ***above all***. In other words whatever you do, please don't forget this one. Like the slogan for American Express, "don't leave home without it," don't leave home without your shield of faith. The shield can be used to protect any area, because it's flexible, workable. The example given is that you will be able to quench all the fiery darts of the wicked. It works for you, it soaks out the fiery darts. It's a super soaker. Check out Hebrews 11; the entire chapter is a memoir of faith, what it does, how it works, what it looks like, how it is applied. Now faith, right now faith!

Helmet of Salvation

The helmet covers the head and brain. It covers the ears and, in some instances, the eyes. We must not let our thoughts be infiltrated with those of the imps of satan. Without the helmet, the gates of our being are left exposed: HEAD, EARS and EYES. Our thoughts, what we hear and what we see. Are these not some of the same tools he used on Eve in the garden? When satan sends a poison dart to your thoughts (the head), don't entertain it; immediately cast it out, and remind the devil that those are his thoughts and not yours and you will have nothing to do with them.

2 Cor 10:5 Casting down imaginations, and every high thing that exalteth itself against the knowledge of God, and bringing into captivity every thought to the obedience of Christ;

Maybe it's just me, but have you ever gotten the weirdest thoughts, most foul, unrepeatable thoughts at the beginning of prayer, while fasting, in the middle of a conversation and say to yourself, "Where in

Basic Training

the world did that come from?" You and I both know exactly where, and who those thoughts came from. But let me tell you what the bible says: (James 4:7) Resist the devil and he will (authors emphasis ***must***) flee. Remind the enemy that you have the mind of Christ (I Corinthians 2:16), you have a transformed mind (Romans 12:2), then remind yourself of the fact (Ephesians 4:23) that you are to be renewed, in the spirit of your mind. (Translation: You've got a new mental attitude, a new way of thinking, no more stinking, thinking.

We must not let our eyes be blinded, nor our ears tainted by the enemy. Here's a key fact: satan uses people, even the born again Christians (if we're not careful). Let me show you how he works. You over hear as my mom would say; the tail end of a conversation in which you thought you heard your name mentioned. He's what the enemy will do: He will plant a thought in your head that obviously the person that you overheard does not like you. Here's what he wants us to do: Build up animosity and dislike, because of something you thought you heard. Send the devil his message back and tell him it was undeliverable, you can't receive it, because it doesn't belong to you. Let me just mention this while we're here: If you did hear someone saying something about you that's untrue, the bible says, "Blessed are ye when men... shall say all manner of evil against you falsely for my sake." (Matthew 5:11 Key word ***falsely***. ***If it is true***, don't get angry, get better- it's the truth).

Remember the enemy will use anybody and anything. The scripture says, And ***take*** the helmet, translation from the Greek, take means *receive*. Accept the helmet, it's for your own good.

Sword of the Spirit/Word of God

This is your offensive weapon and we'll deal with this in chapter 5 "Know your weapons".

Power of Prayer

Pray is a powerful tool and a great weapon against the enemy. It is a tool that can be used anytime of the day or night. Prayer changes things. Let's call a witness. Hezekiah tell us what happen to you.

Isaiah 38:1-5 In those days was Hezekiah sick unto death. And Isaiah the prophet the son of Amoz came unto him, and said unto him, Thus saith the LORD, Set thine house in order: for thou shalt die, and not live. Then Hezekiah turned his face toward the wall, and prayed unto the LORD,

And said, Remember now, O LORD, I beseech thee, how I have walked before thee in truth and with a perfect heart, and have done that which is good in thy sight. And Hezekiah wept sore. Then came the word of the LORD to Isaiah, saying, Go, and say to Hezekiah, Thus saith the LORD, the God of David thy father, I have heard thy prayer, I have seen thy tears: behold, I will add unto thy days fifteen years.

Basic Training

Of course we know pray is a way of communicating with our Heavenly Father. Prayer is not an occasional thing when situations occur. Prayer is a life style. God's ears are open to prayer. I agree with E.M. Bounds, the author who says; "prayer opens a limitless storehouse and God's hand withholds nothing, when we pray. Pray with power and purpose. (See more about prayer in chapter 5)

Early Morning Regimen

In basic training there is something called daily or early morning regimen (EMR), after which there is roll call. These are two extremely important areas that should not be overlooked.

Military service personnel, no matter what line of defense, participate in **EMR**; this may seem like routine, hard work, but actually the body is being awakened, becoming energized, and the blood is beginning to flow. Proper exercise builds strong bodies and muscle, strong triceps, biceps and calves, etc. The same concept and principle applies in your *early morning spiritual regimen*. If you have not done so, start right away, whether you feel like it or not, get up!

What is an **EMSR**? That's when you, wake up by the grace of God, go into prayer by the power of God, read His Word by the anointing of Holy Ghost and then praise and worship the Most High God, Jehovah-Elohim, because He is worthy.

Spend time conversing, with the Lord, in your audible voice and/or in your heavenly language.

Every day can't be a "deep" Bible study. But every day you can study a little bit, even if only for a few minutes. Finally, pause/Salah and listen— now you're in roll call: listen for your assignment, as you leave your barracks, your place of rest and refuge, your home, you must apply the Blood of Jesus.

If you fail to complete your *early morning spiritual regimen* you will find the spiritual body will grow weak, the spirit man will grow weak and sluggish and your mind will not be focused. You will be unprepared, your hearing will be clogged and you won't run like you used to. Your appetite changes, the Blood flow is clogged and the connection is loose. Your muscles are not as tight. You get it?

Please don't misunderstand the meaning of regimen. Although it may appear routine, mundane or religious, it's not if you're sincere. Married men and women (my brothers and sisters), do you spend time with your mate because it's a routine? Do you talk with your children because you have to? Is it a routine, chore or task? Neither should your set aside time with the Lord be any different. He's your Father, and he wants you in good shape.

Basic Training

Work Page II—RECRUIT: List the books of the Bible in order

	ISAIAH	
NUMBERS		
		COLOSSIANS
	JONAH	
1 CHRONICLES		
		1 JOHN
PSALMS		
	ACTS	

Chapter III

R&R: Rank and Responsibility

The U.S. Army has ten enlisted ranks. In the Lord's army, the initial rank is disciple or servant of Christ. It makes no difference what previous training you have come into this army with or where you received your Ph.D., doctrinal degree or from what seminary you graduated. There is only one rank you need be concerned with, your commands come from the Trinity: God the Father, God the Son, God the Holy Ghost.

Philippians 2:10-11 That at the name of Jesus every knee shall bow ...11: and that every tongue should confess that Jesus Christ is Lord.

Marilyn Hickey's book ***Devils, Demons and Deliverance***, the author writes "Just as there is a hierarchy in the U.S. Army, there is a rank and file in satan's army. satan is the commander in chief, followed by what are known as devils- the generals, captains, and lieutenants; demons- the sergeant majors, staff sergeant majors, and first sergeants; and evil spirits- the privates and those who have received few, if any stripes." Hickey goes on to say "For every move that the devil makes, God has a countermove. For every power play maneuver, strategy, or evil attack that satan may attempt to launch against you, God has given you a counter attack that will put the devil on his back and his demon powers fleeing from you in fear." (Hallelujah!)

"The most important thing you can remember is that you are a child of God and are protected from the wiles of the enemy. God told you that because He loves you, No weapon that is formed against thee shall prosper."

Disciples

A disciple is a learner, a pupil, one who studies to learn from another (the ways) and proceeds to put them into action, a follower.

If you look at the original biblical disciples, that's exactly what they did. If you look a little closer, you will find that they were ordinary folks just like you and I; however, they were willing to trust Jesus, the Christ, the Anointed One.

I once heard someone describe the disciples as primarily a bunch of thieves, thugs and cutthroats. What qualified them to be used of God? It's simple: Their *desire* to be used by God, their willingness to become obedient and, if necessary, even to their death. Jesus qualified us, He and only He.

Colossians 1:12 (AMP) **Giving thanks to the Father, Who has *qualified* and made us fit to share the portion which is the inheritance of the saint (God's holy people) in the Light.**

Militant Spirit

A Christian disciple should know something about war and being persistent. Have you ever known a spiritual sister or brother with a militant teaching spirit. To have a militant spirit means to be an aggressive soldier, with a crusading zeal, engaged in warfare or combat: a fighting spirit, aggressive, active in a cause, maybe even combative.

Always on the look out
Always looking out for an opportunity not to fight **but to teach** others, confront, detect and beat down the strong holds of ignorance.

Always on spiritual attack
Ready to attack the enemy (not others); be careful you don't begin attacking the troopers in the same army with you. You'll hear more about this Friendly Fire in Chapter III. Attack dumb spirits, false teachings, cults and witchcraft and the spirit of error. Read more about this under Binding and Loosing in Chapter V.

Always marching or stepping high
Stepping high over adversities, the enemy, stepping over defeat.

Always ready
1 Peter 3:15 But sanctify the Lord God in your hearts: and <u>be ready</u> always to give an answer to every man that asketh you a reason of the hope that is in you with meekness and fear:

Always prepared with your weapons
Know what weapons you have and be prepared to use them. What good is it to know them and have them dusty sitting on a shelf? Pick your weapons up and use them: the Name of Jesus, the Blood of Jesus, Prayer, Praise, the Word of God and your heavenly language.

Whatever area God has assigned you, you'll notice a militant spirit. Don't become alarmed, it's called an apostolic anointing; you'll hear more about that later.

Work the Work

If your ministry Is Evangelism
You will evangelize anywhere. All of us have been called to be a witness, but when the militant spirit of evangelism is your calling, the demand on your "draft" comes into full view, and you operate on automatic. You will witness:

In the store, on the street corner, in the salon, at school, in the doctor's office, at the bus stop, at the bank, etc.

And you'll be militant about it: Nobody can stop you; it's deeply embedded within you. You can't turn it off, you can't turn it on, it's always there and if you could help it, you would, but you can't- it oozes out like perspiration from a runner in a 5k marathon. You can't hold the "sweat" back, and you can't hold the witness back.

If your ministry is Music

You will sing and praise God anywhere: In a crowd area, all alone, on stage or in an elevator; in a church with nine-thousand or in a room with only nine. You will teach it in song, you preach it in song, you'll pray it in song. In your head you hear sweet melodies and tunes; Holy Ghost gives you words, He even sings to you. If we check out your room, or private quarters we will find: workbooks, scratch pads, notes and scraps of paper with songs and words. As He pours into you, you are compelled to write it down, sing it into a tape, repeat it in your head, play it on an instrument, or hum it in your head! When in spiritual warfare, you hear militant war tunes and beats. You visualize marching, waving fist, and battle cries. You don't ask for it, but you are compelled by this passion for God, and His passion and love that He has placed in you.

Understand my brothers and sisters, you're a different kind of **prisoner of war (POW) (see chapter IV)**

Ephesians 4:1 I therefore, the prisoner of the Lord, beseech you that ye walk worthy of the vocation wherewith ye are called.

A Metamorphosis

At the age of about thirteen, *when I begin to think I was practically grown*, I began to see the metamorphosis of John 1:14 in my life, "the Word was made flesh." I actually experienced the Word becoming flesh, real *in my life. Jesus became more than a story out of the Bible, He became the living Word in my life.* We all must come to a place in our lives where we can actually see, feel and/or sense the mighty move of God in our lives. A metamorphosis does in fact take place. No it may not be like the old spiritual hymn that says, "looked at my hands and they looked new, looked at my feet and they did too!" Here's a metamorphosis news flash: It ain't gonna' happen like that for everybody. If you heard and saw all the wonderful things just mentioned, great; but if you didn't, take note, that doesn't mean God is not moving in your life. But, you should be able to see a change. You shouldn't be in the same place (spiritually) that you were in 1985, in 1998, or last year; there should be a change.

Seed Planting in the Middle of a War

I'm no great horticulturist or farmer, but the little I *do* know about planting is once the ground has been prepared and the seed planted, even though I don't see with the naked eye a change taking place, that does not mean that beneath the dirt there's nothing taking place. But after a while, I can see for myself, a bud, a sprout, a sign of growth that will eventually bloom and blossom into something big and beautiful. Even in a war, seeds must be planted. It does no good for you to eat up all the seeds, once you've caught the vision, caught on to the fact that you need to sow into the lives of others.

As a matter of fact, the Bible actually talks about there being a process in planting. Seedtime and Harvest.

1 Corinthians 3:6 I have planted, Apollos watered; but God gave the increase.

We are laborers together with God, sowing seeds.

Beyond Basic Training

There are many characteristic's and traits you can think of when describing a teacher and identifying what a teacher does. There are things a teach needs and doesn't need. (See chart on page 56.)

Think of a few characteristics you have that will help in your teaching assignment. Now think of those you desire. Ask yourself, why do I desire this? Your answer must be for the Glory of God in your teaching ministry. Otherwise, we've got to go back to the drawing board to rid ourselves of selfish gain. Remember, it's all about God, and that He will get the glory and praise.

NEEDS	NEEDS	NEEDS	NOT NEEDED
A teacher needs a student to impart	A prayer life	Discipline to study	A teacher does not need to be a great speaker
A teacher needs a listener to impart	A love for God's people	A desire to learn	Doesn't need to know big words
A teacher needs a good follower to impart	To live life by example	A desire to share the Gospel	Does not make others feel less because you know so much

Your Company, Your Platoon

I remember years ago, hearing a secular teacher (teacher by profession) make a statement about teaching that stayed in my mind throughout the years. When asked to state her profession, the teacher responded, "I teach children." I found it so interesting that she did not respond like the average person, by indicating, that she taught third grade math or tenth grade English. Instead she said, "I teach **children**." If someone were to ask you, right now today, what you do in the ministry, what would your response be? "I teach adults age twenty-five and up?" "I teach new members?" Or would you say, I teach people!"

Can you see the vision is much broader than you could have imagined? Can you count God's people? No! Can you put a limit on God's authority? No! His power? No! His purpose in your life? No! Then don't limit Him in the ministry He has called you into. Get His world wide vision in your mind and you will say, "It's bigger than that." **Eyes hath not seen neither hath ears heard the things that God....** Get a greater, broader vision. Say it, "I teach God's people." Now understand, this assignment is a great responsibility; it is representative of Him.

It's important that we come to understand rank and responsibility. For one to be responsible, simply put, means to be accountable and faithful. Let me give you an example. You go to work each day, you have a responsibility on that job and/or to your employer. Your job or employer has a responsibility to you and that is to pay you. Parents have a responsibility to their children: to provide for them and raise them. But, you and I both know that all parents are not responsible parents. Some are strung out on crack cocaine, some drink up their children's book supply money on alcohol. Just because you wear the title of "Parent" does not mean you have accepted and are fulfilling the role, rank and responsibility of being a parent. Whatever your area of ministry, be accountable. Even when we mess up, Jehovah Jireh is a wonderful provider. He swears by His name, and He is faithful. Let's you and I strive to be faithful like our Father.

What a Compliment

It has been said that teachers who have been called by God have received a great compliment from Him, by Him bestowing such a title upon you. He has called you to teach HIS Word! Teaching the Word of God to someone- anyone- is exciting. The fact that God allows us, such fallible human beings, to teach His Word is a privilege beyond measure. You and I both can probably speak from experience, if it were left up to us we would mess it up. But, thanks be unto God who gives us the victory and who gave us the Holy Ghost as our teacher (John 14:26).

That scripture does not imply that you are not held accountable for your teaching. That's where the study part comes in. The Holy Ghost can only bring back to your remembrance that which you have put in. It's almost like a bank account, if you put money in, you can draw money out. But if you've not put anything in, what are you drawing on?

Our Father holds us responsible for teaching a clear, biblically-sound lesson and we must present it, knowing we're in His presence.

The Bible clearly indicates the responsibility of teaching. Not everyone possesses the gift of teaching, as stated in the New Testament.

Ephesians 4:11 And he gave some, apostles; and some, prophets; and some, evangelists; and some, pastors and teachers;

No where in the Word of God does it say He gave *all* teachers. Some are called to do other works, but everyone should know how to witness. It may not be in the classroom, but how about the barber shop, the bus stop or in the shopping mall? Some will be apostles, who should know how to witness, some will be prophets, who should know how to witness; every evangelist and pastor should know how to dissect the Word and witness.

Paul instructed Timothy, to study.

2 Timothy 2:15 Study to shew thyself approved unto God, a workman that needeth not to be ashamed, rightly dividing the word of truth.

The studying is to show thyself approved unto God. However, we often overlook the scriptures which follow, which are just as important as the former:

16 But shun profane and vain babblings: for they will increase unto more ungodliness.

17 And their word will eat as doth a canker: of whom is Hymenaeus and Philetus;

18 Who concerning the truth have erred, saying that the resurrection is past already; and overthrow the faith of some.

19 Nevertheless the foundation of God standeth sure, having this seal, The Lord knoweth them that are his. And, Let every one that nameth the name of Christ depart from iniquity.

20 But in a great house there are not only vessels of gold and of silver, but also of wood and of earth; and some to honour, and some to dishonour.

21 If a man therefore purge himself from these, he shall be a vessel unto honour, sanctified,

and meet for the master's use, and prepared unto every good work.

Let's look at that. In verses 16-18, to *shun* means to avoid, keep away from, have nothing to do with; *profane* means not fit for the place of worship; and *vain babbling*, is to speak false words and false doctrine- fruitless talk that destroys the soul like gangrene until nothing is left, until spiritual death is reaped. Remember Hymenalus and Philetus both taught in error by saying the resurrection was past, but it hadn't; their careless teaching destroyed the faith of others, precious souls were deceived.

Verse 19 says that, God's truth is a sure foundation no matter how others intentionally or unintentionally mess it up. It will stand sure. So teachers you must, study and teach the truth. Never forget the Lord knows those who are his.

Verse 20 illustrates how in a great house, there's gold, silver and also wood and earth; some will honor and some will dishonor. We have all different kinds of teachers; some glitter (as my Mom would say, "All that glitters is not gold"); some will honor and some will not.

Verse 21 urges a man to purge himself or get rid of, keep himself clean of those things listed in this chapter so that he will be a vessel sanctified, fit for the master's use. There are seven particular areas we are referring to in this chapter:

1. Affairs of this life
2. Backsliding
3. Unbelief

R&R: Rank and Responsibility

---

4. False doctrine that destroys faith
5. Profane and vain and babblings that lead to ungodliness
6. False teachings that overturn an individual's faith
7. All iniquity (sin) and dishonor

Verse 22 says run from youthful lust's follow after righteousness, faith, love and peace along with those who call on the Lord out of a pure heart.

Then Peter tells us in **1 Peter 3:15** "Sanctify (set aside) Christ as Lord in your hearts, always being ready to make a defense (back up what you believe) to everyone who asks you to give the reason for the hope that you have. But make sure you do this with gentleness and reverence." (author interpretation)

(NIV) But in your hearts set apart Christ as Lord. Always be prepared to give an answer to everyone who asks you to give the reason for the hope that you have. But do this with gentleness and respect.

Now, **2 Timothy 2:2** And the things which thou hast heard from me among many witnesses, the same commit thou to faithful men, who shall be able to teach others also...(ASV)

Over and over again, the New Testament imperative rings; the Word of God must be taught by *faithful* teachers to *faithful* listeners.

You're going to hear **2 Timothy.2:15** over and over again, so let it get in your spirit now. Accurately handle the word of truth!

Paul also urged Titus:

See Titus 2:1 But speak thou the things which

become sound doctrine: (Speak the things which are fitting for good teaching).

Finally the urgency of the responsibility is summed up in **James 3,** The teacher is responsible for what and how he teaches.

James 3:1 My brethren, be not many masters, knowing that we shall receive the greater condemnation.

Oh yes, teaching is a BIG JOB. But it's God's job. How blessed you are to share in it! Your responsibility is to teach the truth. satan will tell you how under qualified you are and that's okay; he may think so, but it's not the truth. You can do all things through Christ who strenthens you. We've listed the characteristics and attributes of a teacher, and glanced at the qualifications.

What does it take to qualify you as a teacher? This is one of the first exercises we should complete in our Teacher Training Classes. Complete the following list.

WORK PAGE III —RECRUIT

Begin to think about the scriptures which describe, direct, instruct and proclaim what teacher's should teach. I'll give you a few hints. Drop in prayer, open your Bible and complete this page. Use your concise Concordance if needed.

1. I must hold fast to sound doctrine.
   2 Tim. 1:13
2. I am charged to teach no other doctrine, neither give heed to fables.....
   1 Tim 1:3-4

3.

4.

5.

6.

7.

8.

WORK PAGE IV—Recruit: Drop and give me 10

Find 10 scriptures that speak to you about being faithful. **Matthew 25:21 His lord said unto him, Well done, thou good and faithful servant: thou hast been faithful over a few things, I will make thee ruler over many things: enter thou into the joy of thy lord.**

1.

2.

3.

4.

5.

6.

7.

8.

9.

10.

Now give God praise because He is worthy.

Chapter IV

Know Your Weapons

Over the years I've found the weapons in the U.S. military have changed. The U.S. Armed Forces use all different types of weapons and equipment to carry out the commands and combat missions of the Commander and Chief. Weapons were used for defense and for offensive measures. The United States history of wars began with the Revolutionary War in 1775-1783 this is where we get the history of the Lexington, Concord and Bunker Hill battles.*

- The Civil War in 1861 included battles such as Bull Run, Shiloh and Gettysburg.
- Word War I in 1917; the war actually began in 1914, but the United States did not enter until 1917.

- World War II in 1939
- 1950 the Korean War (which my paternal father fought)
- 1954 the Vietnam War
- 1991 we joined the Gulf War
- 2001 Operation Enduring Freedom

The purpose of listing each war or giving war history was simply to explain that in each war there was a key weapon, and each weapon was different from that of the previous war.

As part of my search and research, many hours were spent in the library studying books from every level on military operations and war. I checked out every video tape I could find on the market in relation to wars.

Again in different wars there were different weapons:

There were nuclear weapons, this type of weapon gets its destructive power from the transformation of matter in atoms into energy.

Biological weapons are those which spread disease among people quicker than the common cold.

Chemical biological radiological warfare (CBR) is when war is waged with chemicals, biological agents or radioactive materials. I just don't believe George Washington or Abe Lincoln knew anything about chemical warfare, but I believe they knew how to use the weapons of their day. -canons and marching men.

*I intentionally left out some battles, not by lack of importance, but I did not want this book to turn into a history text book but rather provide interesting and truthful information. I am grateful for every battle fought and every victory won. Please consult your local library for additional historical information.

The point of bringing this up is that the enemy (satan) will use anybody to persuade them to become his tool and weapon. Be careful, be very careful he uses Christian's too. Gasp! Shocker! Yes, he does if you let him.

A lie is just like a *Biological/nuclear* weapon; it is destructive whether big or small. Once the destructive power is unleashed, it passes on, and on and on; this is how the enemy feeds and get strong. He has no power except what we render to him.

You have been equipped to disarm the bomb, the weapon, by not passing it on. Put it out, stop it from going any further.

Lust of the flesh is just like a *Chemical biological radiological* warfare (CBR). When war is waged with fleshly sin, it is passed on as a generational curse, from generation to generation. Rather than stop it, you accept it and say, I knew it would rise. My sisters and brothers, chop it off at the knee. Kill it, do not let sin reign.

POW's

During the Korean War, there was a cruel treatment developed to change the method of thinking for Prisoners of War. My heart goes out to the men and women who not only fought in this war but endured the bullying and barbaric treatment sustained as a POW. This particular treatment was called Brainwashing. POW's were subjected to systematic indoctrination intended to undermine allegiance to their country. Did you know that satan does the same thing? He captures your attention, tries to lock you down as a prisoner in your own mind, then he consistently fills your head with repetitious thoughts to infiltrate your mind and attempt to brainwash you into thinking you are less than who and what God says you are. You cannot allow him to take over.

Here's what he does: he shoots fiery darts at you countless numbers at a time; he is just hoping that one will hit the spot and start a fire- remember these are fiery darts. Eph 6:16 says .....ye shall be able to quench all the fiery darts of the wicked, if you are wearing your fatigues. This is why it is so important that you wear your battle "Fatigues" your uniform and/or armour. Let's look at your entire **UNIFORM** again.

Ephesians 6:16 Finally, my brethren, be strong in the Lord, and in the power of his might. Put on the whole armour of God, that ye may be able to stand against the wiles of the devil.

For we wrestle not against flesh and blood, but against

principalities, against powers, against the rulers of the darkness of this world, against spiritual wickedness in high places. Wherefore take unto you the whole armour of God, that ye may be able to withstand in the evil day, and having

done all, to stand. Stand therefore, having your loins girt about with truth, and having on the breastplate of righteousness; And your feet shod with the preparation of the gospel of peace; Above all, taking the shield of faith, wherewith ye shall be able to quench all the fiery darts of the wicked. And take the helmet of salvation, and the sword of the Spirit, which is the word of God: Praying always with all prayer and supplication in the Spirit, and watching thereunto with all perseverance and supplication for all saints;**

The Weapons of our Warfare

The Bible teaches us that the weapons of our warfare are not carnal (2 Corinthians 10:4); in other words, our weapons are out of this world. How is that you ask? Because our weapons are spiritual and cannot be seen. Our weapons can't be beat. What are our weapons? I'm glad you asked.

The Word of God says our weapons are (mighty through God) powerful and great and the purpose is to (pull down strong holds) cause destruction to areas that have been exalted, areas like "religion," not relationship but religion. You can religiously take an aspirin each day for your health. This is what religion means: to be repetitious and do something over and over again. To have a relationship is to love, appreciate, cherish and sacrifice. Aren't these all attributes Jesus demonstrated towards us in that while we were yet sinners He died for us? He demonstrated his love in action, He had compassion for us, He sacrificed for us and He did it all for relationship. Good God, what manner of Love!!! Hallelujah!

Fight with the Sword, not a Butter Knife

I grew up in a family of five children, two boys and three girls. At this particular time in my life, money (to the children) was not of importance. We never realized what we didn't have. Even when it came to tools in the house. Either we didn't have them, or I didn't know where they were. So, thus, the need and purpose of a butter knife: It was used for everything. To cut with, as a screw driver, the butt end as a hammer, to curl ribbon for gifts, occasionally to cut, butter.

Some of us are pulling out a butter knife to fight the enemy rather than our Sword. The butter knife won't even nick the enemy. The butter knife mentality is "playing with the devil, our adversary." When we play with him, we really, really don't want him out or totally gone, we just want him to stop bothering us right now, for this minute. Do we realize when he leaves and then returns, he will come back seven times stronger? Unfortunately, some of us let him in and don't realize the damage we are doing to ourselves.

I say today, we must wage war on the enemy. Kill him and don't shed a tear at the funeral- let him go.

Now here's what the enemy will do: He'll send another situation, another problem, another heartache, another whatever, but different spirits, to oppress you and try to wear you down. This is why we must know our weapons and how to use them.

What are Our Weapons

Normally one would think you don't need weapons in a teaching capacity, but you must be ready for this attack. Our weapons are:

Prayer
In your native tongue or your heavenly tongue, this is so important that we cannot overlook the power of prayer. At Valley Kingdom Ministries International, Apostle H. Daniel Wilson launched a Holy Ghost-lead project titled "Operation JERICHO." Hundreds of Christians went to the downtown Chicago area and prayed for our city, mayor, political leaders, neighbors, etc. We pulled down every stronghold we could think of. Another team went to a specific area, which included our cities Financial District and Sears Tower. They prayed in the worst inclement weather; a huge storm arose, but they continued to pray *in the* storm. I believe beyond the shadow of a doubt that the very reason those buildings are still standing today, is because somebody prayed. (See more about prayer in chapter II)

Praise
Thanking God for everything. Give thanks in all things, for this is the will of the Father. Feel free to

allow the Holy Spirit to invite you to enter in, to be ushered into the presence of our God by worshiping and listening to Praise and Worship music. At the end of this book, I recommend many tapes and CD's that will bless you as you enter into your private praise and worship.

The Word of God

This is your Sword. The Bible says Heaven and earth will pass away, but the Word of God will stand forever. God swears by His Word. He commands His Word to not return to Him void. His Word is not going to come back to Him and say, sorry, couldn't do what you told me to do. That's good news. Begin to learn a new scripture ever week, that's fifty -two in one year's time. Prepare yourself, hide His word in your heart that you won't sin against God.

The Blood of Jesus

Nothing can penetrate the Blood of Jesus. In war you must expect blood. Don't be afraid to get blood on your hands, ears, mouth- just become a bloody mess! But the blood I speak of must be applied, ask Jesus to cover you with His Blood, so that the enemy can't hurt you.

The Fruit of the Spirit

Somehow fruit just doesn't seem to fit into the weapon category, but, have you ever heard of a Food Fight? This one is permitted without detention.

Galatians 5:22-23 The fruit of the Spirit is Love, Joy, Peace, Longsuffering, Gentleness,

Goodness, Faith, Meekness, Temperance: against such there is no law.

The Enemy's Weapons

Not only is it important that *you know* your weapons: but you better know the weapons that the *enemy* will use. One of the key factors in losing a battle is lack of knowledge. My mother says you know better, so you do better. The Bible says

Hosea 4:6 My people are destroyed for lack of knowledge.

Four Foul rebels

Paul helps us to be mindful of the enemy (satan) and his cohorts in the book of Ephesians; I call them the four foul rebels. We wrestle against **principalities,** satan's generals who oversee entire nations (see Daniel chapter 10); against **powers**, his privates who possess human beings (see Mark 5 and Matthew 17) and they carry out the orders of their chief ruler; against the **rulers of the darkness** *of this world*, demons in charge of satan's worldly business; against **spiritual wickedness**, demons in charge of *worldly religion* and wickedness in the heavenlies/high places.

Look back at Ephesians 6:11, "that ye may be able to stand against the wiles of the devil." What are the wiles? Wiles in the Greek is a word know as *methodeia*, it refers to the cunning arts, deceit, crafty, trickery *methods.* The different means, plans, schemes used to deceive, entrap, enslave and ruin the souls of men. When we sin, it becomes ammunition for the devil to do damage. It's like opening a gate and letting his troops in, keep in mind we open the gate for not just one, but the entry becomes open access. It makes no difference if we just slightly crack the gate open, open is open. How do we open the gate? Glad you asked, through sin and failure to repent and confess our sins.

2 Corinthians 10:3,5 For though we walk in the flesh, we do not war after the flesh... Casting down imaginations, and every high thing that exalteth itself against the knowledge of God, and bringing into captivity every thought to the obedience of Christ;

Romans 8:6 For to be carnally minded is death; but to be spiritually minded is life and peace.

Romans 10:10 For with the heart man believeth unto righteousness; and with the mouth confession is made unto salvation.

The Enemy's Weapons II

We already know that we are victors and not victims, but we must be mindful of the devices of the enemy. The battle starts in the mind. He will send thoughts to you that don't belong to you, in the middle of prayer, while listening to music, while reading the Word and you must take every precaution to cast them down.

The enemy will use anything and everything to capture your attention to cause you to focus on him, he wants your attention, praise and your worship. **He**

uses every sin and strongman, both imaginable and unimaginable, every form of trickery and every foul thought.

In Galatians 5:19-21, the works of the flesh are: Adultery, fornication, uncleanness, lasciviousness (eagerness for lustful pleasure), idolatry, witchcraft, hatred, wrath, strife, sedition (the feeling that everyone else is wrong except those in your own little group), heresies, envying, murder, drunkenness. Don't forget the spirit of infirmity, fear, lust, bondage, idolatry, heaviness, perverse spirits, murmuring, hatred, lies, jealousy, error, violent thoughts, violence against property, etc.

For every temptation of sin and strongman sent our way, we have a counteractive solution. See page 82.

Flee or Fight

Once you realize the enemy's weapon is sin and the temptation of sin, you will know how to deal with it. If the enemy stands right in front of you, waving his fist, that's all he's done. No licks or hits have been passed. Growing up on the west side of Chicago, if you were going to fight, first of all everybody knew it was going to be a fight- somehow the word got out. A part of the strategy was to determine in advance if you were going to run or fight. Some battles are not worth your time, and others you may need to flee.

Let me give you an example. You could put me in

a room full of crack cocaine and alcohol, and it would not tempt me in any way. This is not a battle for me. I don't have to bind or loose anything because I can walk away without a fight. On the other hand, leave me in a bakery or candy store, and "Houston we have a problem," there may be a struggle- I need to run from this fight, in other words get up, flee, change my environment. If I'm not in a position to leave, I must learn to put my flesh under subjection to what I say.

Encourage Yourself

In a fight, before a fight and even after a fight you've got to know how to encourage yourself. Learn to build up yourself, your strength to get back in the battle. Before Goliath came along David needed to be encouraged.

As a shepherd he was exposed to wild beasts, he probably study the enemy that was after the sheep. Rather than give up and say those lions and bears have too many sharp teeth, he decided, I can do this! How do I know that? Remember in I Samuel 17:34 David explained how a lion and a bear came and took a lamb; in verse 35 He says he went after them and took the lamb out of the beast mouth. He was going to let the animal at least live, but he rose up on him and the bible says he caught him by his beard and smote him and slew both the lion and the bear.

He was encouraging himself. So when it came to Goliath who was almost ten feet tall, David believed he could do this. Not only did he have confidence but he knew that God was and is able.

You may have a few lion, bears and even Goliath in your life, but you must encourage yourself, believe and know that God is able. Look at what David told his enemy.

1 Sam 17:45 Then said David to the Philistine, Thou comest to me with a sword, and with a spear, and with a shield: but I come to thee in the name of the LORD of hosts, the God of the armies of Israel

Beyond Just Knowing

satan doesn't want you to see the Savior, Jesus the Christ. He doesn't care that sinners believe in God, believing in God alone is no proof that you are justified by faith or have accepted Christ as Lord and Savior, for even devils believe without justification (James 2:19). We must teach to go beyond just knowing Him and receiving salvation, you must want more. We must be willing to come out of our comfort zone and share with others the Gospel of Jesus Christ, by any means necessary. The beginning steps must be to win the very "members" in our churches, class rooms, homes, neighborhood, communities, district, city, suburbs, county, state, country and ultimately the world.

Cross Fire

We must be ever mindful of who and whose we

are. We are winners, victorious, prophets and priests, we're royalty, a holy nation, blessed, highly favored, spirit filled, sanctified, believers, children of God, we are loved of God, we are partakers of Christ, we are blessed, we are over comers and so much more. And don't you ever forget it! We are not our own, we don't belong even to our own self:

1 Cor 6:19 says "What? know ye not that your body is the temple of the Holy Ghost which is in you, which ye have of God, and ye are not your own?

We must know *whose we are*.

Our goal as Christians in a war is to defeat the enemy, cancel his plan, shoot him down, to annihilate (destroy all traces of) the enemy and his plans to destroy. In this book we study how we can eliminate, what are our weapons, how to be victorious seed sowers, etc. Here's even better news "satan is a defeated foe and the WAR is already won." What you may face is an individual battle. I know there are many Bible scholars who will say, "The battle is not yours, it's the Lord's." Perhaps this is true in many individual battles that you are faced with, but I'm speaking of the raging WAR between knowledge and ignorance- baby, you've got to come against this one.

This is serious! As we shoot down the enemy, his cohorts and imps, we've got to be extremely careful that we don't get caught in the cross fire. When you ask God to handle a situation, do you pick it up and put it back down, then pick it up again and again? This is a good way to get hit in the cross fire.

Picture this: You're in the middle of a ranging

battle, shots are being fired back and forth; instead of you following the instructions of the commander and chief to get out of the way, you decide to run out and do some things on your own. Chances are you're going to get hit in the cross fire. It was unnecessary and could have been avoided, but you chose to do it your way. Do you understand what I'm saying? When God tells you to stay our of the way, no matter how helpful you want to be, stay out of the way! When God says he's got this one, let him have it!

Friendly Fire

Here's another unpleasant subject, but we've got to deal with. Who want's to be known for shooting down their partner? No one! My dear Christian brothers and sisters, let's not forget who the real enemy is. It's not the pastor, the choir director or the church secretary; we're all on the same team. I know, it may not always seem like it, but that's why you've got to wear "night vision glasses" called ***discernment***. You must be able to see past the dark, past the hurt, past the "they did me wrong," past the "I know they don't like me," so you can see who is the real enemy. Don't take it out on your brothers and sisters." This is friendly fire that damages our brothers and sisters spirit, and God hates it.

Proverbs 6:19... he that soweth discord among brethren.

Friendly fire is discharged when we see something that appears to be a threat and we act upon it, without checking with the "Watch Commander" (Holy Spirit). We end up shooting down one another and that's discord. There is a book I use over and over again as a tool to keep my discernment tools sharp. It's titled ***Stongman's His Name, What's His Game?*** by Jerry and Carol Robeson, a very powerful study tool in the area of spiritual warfare and discernment, very easy reading and application.

I told you earlier that the enemy doesn't care who he uses, but we must understand that we can hate the sin but not the sinner. The Bible says that (all of us) **"have sin and come short of the glory of God. (Romans 3:23)**

And then Galatians 6:1 tells us that if (and we more than likely will) find our brother (at some point or another) over taken in a fault (did or doing something wrong) We who are spiritual (the saints, the Christian) are the ones that should open our arms and help them, forgive them. The Word doesn't tell us to shoot them down, nor to kill 'em. Christ forgave you didn't He? Why can't you forgive your brothers and sisters. This is where we learn to pray all the more. This is where the rubber meets the road, where you see the real Christ in you is revealed- not so much as you lifting hands in praise and dancing in the aisles on Sunday (understand I love to praise, worship and run as much as the next person), but after everybody has gone into their separate homes, what happens on Monday? Allow Holy Spirit to use you to speak an encouraging word or a word in season.

Isaiah 50:4

4   The Lord GOD hath given me the tongue

of the learned, that I should know how to speak a word in season to him that is weary:

I've studies the direction of Holy Spirit, I listen to my Heavenly Father and now I am equipped to speak a word of encouragement. Praise God for a seasoned word.

Work Sheet VII—Recruit: Find the counterattack scriptures for these strongmen.

1. Infirmity (Luke 13:11-13)
   _____

2. Rebellion (1 Samuel 15:23)
   _____

3. Spirit of Error (1 John 4:6)
   _____

4. Fear (2 Timothy 1:7)
   _____

5. Bondage (2 Peter 2:19)
   _____

6. Heaviness (Isaiah 61:3)
   _____

7. Haughtiness (Luke 18:11,12)
   _____

8. Perverse spirit (Proverbs 17:20,23)
   _____

9. Lying (2 Thessalonians 2:9-13)
   _____

10. Jealousy (Galatians 5:19)
    _____

Answers on page 103

Chapter VI

Strategies (Part I)

We must not only know our weapons, we must know the enemy and his weapons and devices. Finally, we must have strategies in place to win the battle. We know the outcome of the war is already in our favor. As a matter of fact, it's a fixed fight. Christ saw to it a long time ago that we would win. What are the strategies? What can be put in place to maintain our status on top and eliminate some of the pitfalls and trenches or traps of the enemy?

Exposure and Disarm

One of the easiest ways in a natural war to be caught, hurt or injured, is to make the mistake of exposing yourself. But again, this battle is different, you must tell the enemy what his destiny will be and Expose him and disarm the enemy. **And having dis-**

armed the powers and authorities, he made a public spectacle of them, triumphing over them by the cross. Colossians 2:15 (NIV)

His end will be...

Revelation 20:10 And the devil that deceived them was cast into the lake of fire and brimstone, where the beast and the false prophet are, and shall be tormented day and night for ever and ever.

Understand the enemy wants you to go against the order of the Commander and Chief (Jesus Christ). He wants you to operate out of the will of God. He doesn't want you to develop strategies or reach your destiny. You must expose him for who he really is, a counterfeiter, a liar and the father of lies.

Locking the Gate

We talked briefly about how the enemy wants to come in and take over. He wants to be in complete control; he wants to be worshiped, praised and admired. But he cannot take over unless we let him in; therefore we must understand how the enemy tries to sneak in. There are three ways we want to address.

1. The battle starts in the <u>mind</u>.
2. The <u>eye</u> is an entry way by what you see and how you react.
3. Actual <u>participation</u>. Remember Eve?

Genesis 3:4-6 Now the serpent was more subtil

Strategies (Part 1)

than any beast of the field which the LORD God had made. And he said unto the woman, Yea, hath God said, Ye shall not eat of every tree of the garden?

And the woman said unto the serpent, We may eat of the fruit of the trees of the garden:

But of the fruit of the tree which is in the midst of the garden, God hath said, Ye shall not eat of it, neither shall ye touch it, lest ye die.

And the serpent said unto the woman, Ye shall not surely die:

For God doth know that in the day ye eat thereof, then your eyes shall be opened, and ye shall be as gods, knowing good and evil.

And when the woman *saw* that the tree was good for food, and that it was pleasant to the *eyes*, and a tree to be *desired* to make one wise, she took of the fruit thereof, *and did* eat, and gave also unto her husband with her; and he did eat.

Before we discuss the entry way, let's first ask the question. "Why was she even in a conversation with the enemy?" See, that's what satan wants us to do: talk to him, keep him company. He wants to see if he can capture our attention. When he starts talking tell him to "shut up"!

Now here's what Eve did. First she held a conversation with the serpent, which caused her to begin thinking. Then she saw that the tree was good for food, it was pleasing to the eye. I tell my single brothers and sisters, we have beautiful people all over the world' it's nothing wrong with seeing a beautiful person but the trouble comes when we do a double take, and lose focus on Christ turning our attention to the enemy. Now here comes the mind part: Our thoughts and mind have truly been taken off of the thoughts of God, and we have begun to use our imagination. The Bible tells us to cast it down, but we begin to pick it up and nurse it, handle it, care for it. And finally we want or desire to participate (that's an action word,) become partakers.

A. Mind
B. Eye
C. Participation

When we leave the gate open we are exposing ourselves to various unclean spirits. It's like waving a white flag, saying, "Here I am. Come and get me". Lock the gate and don't let the enemy in

I spoke earlier about watching movies. Some movies are so raunchy until they should be taken off the air: but, understand, it's the enemy's job to introduce you to and entertain you with garbage. Not all movies are garbage, but if you know that you are not strong enough to watch a movie without (literally and mentally tripping), leave it alone!

This is why we must prepare teachers to prepare teachers.

This is why teachers must follow 2 Timothy 2:15; unprepared teachers can take bits of the scripture out of context and drag a lot of people into error right along with them. For example, there is a scripture that tells Peter to take a little wine for thy stomach. In that period and time wine was considered a good medicine to settle the stomach. Taken out of context, a person could use that as a excuse to drink until they are falling off the bar stool.

Be very careful to understand, study and seek the Holy Ghost for accuracy in the scripture. You can mean well and be sincere, but you can be sincerely wrong.

Revelation in The Sword

Holy Spirit has equipped us with what we need to fight the battle; He has given us the insight, foresight and hind sight to see the enemy coming and declare with the Word of God, the sword's power.

Hebrews 4:12 For the word of God is quick, and powerful, and sharper than any two-edged sword, piercing even to the dividing asunder of soul and spirit, and of the joints and marrow, and is a discerner of the thoughts and intents of the heart.

Paul shared with the church at Corthinth:
1 Corinthians 2:10-16 But God hath revealed them unto us by his Spirit: for the Spirit searcheth all things, yea, the deep things of God.

For what man knoweth the things of a man, save the spirit of man which is in him? even so the things of God knoweth no man, but the Spirit of God.

Now we have received, not the spirit of the world, but the spirit which is of God; that we might know the things that are freely given to us of God.

Which things also we speak, not in the words which man's wisdom teacheth, but which the Holy Ghost teacheth; comparing spiritual things with spiritual.

But the natural man receiveth not the things of the Spirit of God: for they are foolishness unto him: neither can he know them, because they are spiritually discerned. But he that is spiritual judgeth all things, yet he himself is judged of no man.

For who hath known the mind of the Lord, that he may instruct him? But we have the mind of Christ.

Strategy I

First be in contact with the Commander and Chief. This may mean that you must sacrifice portions of your time in order to be clear on what the Lord is telling you to do.

You don't always have to announce God's plans to the entire congregation. Some things he gives just to you, they are not meant to tell everyone. Everyone is not happy that you are where you are, not happy with where you are going, so be cautious with developing information. Be in contact with your pastor and/or your covering so that they will know how to pray for you while consulting God on your behalf.

Strategy II

Second, contact your troops. Post a sign to determine who is really interested in sharing the Gospel "for real," through teaching.

Before the first day of Boot Camp class, obtain a list of all of the students who signed up for this class. Call them to ensure they will be present for the first class session. (This way you're not only determining how many will be present but you're getting "foresight" of the students who will be in class.

You may find that out of the one hundred that signed up, maybe only fifty are really serious- bless God no matter what. Don't become alarmed; work diligently with who you have. Again, if you have five or five-hundred, work with them, just the same, they're all important.

Strategy III

Third, know what tools you have to work with. War can be expensive. Know what tools you have and what you will need to purchase.

- Make sure you have a good study Bible.
- Have more than one interpretation. You've got to love King James for it's old world flavor; but more important, you should obtain Hebrew and Greek interpretations. You may want to invest in an Amplified or New International, version but it's not absolutely necessary.

- A Bible dictionary. This really is handy for Word studies and information.
- The Bible on cassette. For all those difficult pronunciations, which can easily be said once you have reviewed them, in advance. Don't get before your student fumbling and bumbling.
- A Strong concordance is really for the serious student. Temporary or non-active disciples will find themselves using it only once in a while. Excellent material, but it does no good just collecting dust on the shelf.
- Maps come in handy when teaching and describing one locations relation to another.
- Feel free to get articles from newspapers that will assist you in presenting the lessons.
- Game shows. I love watching game shows and converting the games into learning sessions for our students.

Strategy IV

Fourth, draw up your plans. Prepare a written plan; even when you think it's not necessary, prepare it anyway. Again, some folks have problems with this. Some preachers have problems with other preachers and/or teachers using notes. How can I say this? Was Holy Spirit with you when he gave you the revelation? If you trust yourself not to mess it up, go for it, but if your confidence is not in you and you trust Jesus and Him alone, prepare.

Look at it this way, Jesus took notes, the disciples

took notes and prepared sixty-six books. Look at it like a lesson plan; you're not reading it from the paper, but you're staying focused. Creating a syllabus is a great place to start. The syllabus explains what we'd like to accomplish, knowing full well that the Holy Ghost has a right to expand wherever He sees fit.

Here is a sample Syllabus and lesson plan. Know what tools you have to work with.

Title of Class

SYLLABUS

Course Description:
Explain what the class is designed to do.

Course Objective:
Explain what the student should know upon the completion of the classes.

Course Text:
What book and Bibles will be required for each student. It is not appropriate to copy materials for handouts, most material is protected by copyright laws.

Class Procedure:
Any special instructions that should apply for each class. Example: Always sign the attendance sheet, be on time, hand in homework at the beginning of class, etc.

Requirements:

Any special class requirement should be listed here. (Example) Each student must attend all classes. Students are allowed one absence. Home work attributes toward 33 percent of your grade.

Class Schedule:

Let students know when and where classes will be held; try to be consistent. Moving around dissimulates and sometimes confuses students.

Strategy V

Introduction

Why are introductions necessary and helpful? It's important that from day one we begin to develop a student/teacher relationship and familiarize yourself with the "teaching level" of your students. Of course you can use any introduction you are comfortable with, but here are a few to break the ice and get you ready to start your own boot camp and training sessions.

Greet your students. Make sure you have an attendance sheet which can be used each week. Ask each student to answer the following questions:

1. What is your name, and are you a member of this Church?
2. What is one fact about you that many people may not know? i.e. hobbies, martial status, etc.)

3. Why did you enroll in this class and/or what do you expect to receive from this class?

Strategy VI

Briefing
On the first day of class after the introduction, review the class syllabus. Allow time for each student to introduce themselves. If time allows give a mini-exercise to determine a little more about your students (i.e. Bible knowledge, ability to pray, commitment level, etc.) Create a who's who from the Bible. Many Christian stores carry youth and adult Bible quiz games. The following are sample questions which could be used to help break the ice.

- What scripture identifies you as a blessing/gift that He gave to the church body? Ephesians _____

- The Bible says that as a boy Jesus was found teaching in the temple. It also says he grew four ways. Name and describe them? (Luke 2)

-

-

-

-

Lesson Plan

Scripture text: What scriptures are used for this lesson?

Title of Lesson: Appropriate lesson title

Lesson Aim/Purpose: What is the main focus of this lesson?

Biblical background study: Background study of scriptures to show what was happening during the time of this lesson text.

Life Application: How is this lesson applied in today's life experiences?

Conclusion: Summary of the lesson

Next week review and/or weekly assignment: Optional

Strategy VII

There area a number of crafts, games, props and puppets, which can be purchased from many of your local Christian book stores.

Chapter V

Strategies (Part II)

If you noticed in every war there was a strategy the civilians may not have known about; but you better believe everyone in the armed forces in rank knew. You may not always understand the plan of God for your life step by step, but know this, Jeremiah 29:11 reminds us that God has a plan for us; Proverbs 19:21 says many are the plans in a man's heart, but it is the Lords purpose THAT PREVAILS (NIV).

We serve a God who not only has purpose, but who is a God of plans and order. Just as the USAF Has different branches.

God's army is organized into branches too.

John 15:2 Every branch in me that beareth not fruit he taketh away: and every branch that beareth fruit, he purgeth it, that it may bring forth more fruit.

Infantry branch

Fights directly with the enemy during ground combat. In the Christian Army this is every born again Christian. You must know that there will be times when you're going to have to stand. No surrender, no retreat- but go forward. You've got a greater army fighting with you. You've got an entire army of angels, heavenly hosts.

Field artillery

U.S. Armed Forces has Field artillery, which support infantry by firing cannons and missiles at enemy targets on land. From a Christian perspective. These are the serious Christians, not just the once-a-week Sunday morning crew, but the ones that take Jesus *home* with them. These are the saints that will stand in agreement with you in prayer and fasting. This is **the evangelist,** a great part of the Field artillery.

Air defense artillery

This branch protects the field artillery and infantry from enemy planes and missiles. This group used guns and shoot missiles at enemy planes. These are the prayer warriors, **and pastors,** the saints of God who will pray all night in prayer watches if necessary (and sometimes it is). They have become so very aware of the attacks, and their discernment must be extremely sharp.

Armor branch

Provides ground support for infantry. This is the **apostle** who sets order and establishes. Soldiers in the armour branch operate tanks, attack tanks and seek targets on land. This group is also the strong deacons in the ministry.

1 Timothy 3:8-10 Likewise must the deacons be grave (honest, worthy of respect), **not double tongued,** (liars) **not given to much wine** (not getting drunk or high), **not greedy of filthy lucre** (not pursing dishonest gains), **holding the mystery of the faith in a pure conscience** (keep a good conscience and be able to demonstrate the mystery of faith). **And let these also first be proved,** (tested); then let them use the office of a deacon , being (worthy of the office and able to keep themselves from being lifted up in pride and falling in the same manner satan did) **being found blameless** (free from evil and reproach).

Aviation branch

Army's air force. Providing air support for the ground forces. I see these are the praise and worship warriors, who worship on their knees and faces daily. They stand giving praises to God with their hands raised and their voices lifted up. When commanded by Holy Ghost they will flow into war battle cries and prophetic songs of victory. The focal point of this branch is to snip out the airway imps before they reach the people of God.

Special forces branch

This branch is responsible for secret missions. I see the special forces as the **Spirit-filled teachers and prophets** who are able to unfold the secret missions by the Word of God. Not everyone can handle such an assignment, but when the mysteries are unfolded, it can be taught, revelation seen and understood- whether through the spoken word, prophetic word, or prophetically sung, but definitely through revelation of the Holy Ghost.

Conclusion

Romans 14:12 So then every one of us shall give account of himself to God.
We must be accountable.
Did you know that God is accountable. Though He does not need to justify what He does or why He does it, with anyone, I've found that He is.
Romans 11:33-36 .(NIV)
Oh, the depth of the riches of the wisdom and knowledge of God! How unsearchable his judgments, and his paths beyond tracing out! Who has known the mind of the Lord? Or who has been his counselor?

Who has ever given to God, that God should repay him? For him and through him and to him are all things. To him be the glory forever! Amen.

God is accountable to God, He does not need to consult with us or explain His ways to us. He is accountable to Himself. You see in Isaiah 45: He says, "By myself I have sworn." The point I make is, God is accountable to God, He backs up His Word with His Word:

Isaiah 55:11 So shall my word be that goeth forth out of my mouth: it shall not return unto me void, but it shall accomplish that which I please, and it shall prosper *in the thing* **whereto I sent it.**

He is honorable and does not change. Oh, if we could have a fraction of that accountability first to God, then to ourselves, and to one another. I know that's a hard pill to swallow when you don't want to answer to anyone. Be accountable and commit to God.

Secondly, we must be honest with and to ourselves. Our own ability to deceive or fool our self is virtually boundless (in other words we can trip); that's why accountability is so necessary. Here's what we do, we seek counsel from our self, we rationalize with our self (on almost everything), we go through reasonable deduction with ourselves, we answer ourselves. This is a worldly thinking process for the average person. But, I ask you today to come out of your level of reasoning and intelligence and move into the supernatural, spiritual higher level of thinking, where God would have you and I to be.

Proverb 3:5 Trust in the LORD with all thine heart; and lean not unto thine own understanding.

Renew your thinking process daily with the Word of God:

Romans 12:2 And be not conformed (or fashioned according to this world), but be ye transformed by the renewing of your mind, That' not a one time deal or shot, it has to be transformed daily- Just like you brush your teeth daily, if you don't any dentist will tell you that your teeth will, decay. So transformation is a daily process, for we must have the mind of Christ. A higher level of thinking:

Philippians 2:5 Let this mind be in you which is also in Christ Jesus.

Seek counsel from God first. He doesn't mind if it's a little issue or a big issue; He wants you to talk to Him.

In your spare time, meditate on Proverbs 21:2&3

All a man's ways seem right to him, but the Lord weights the heart. To do what is right and just is more acceptable to the Lord than sacrifice.

Many people have deceived themselves, thinking that if they offer sacrifice, this will give them the OK for unrighteousness. But if you study this scripture it explains that sacrifices must be offered with repentance and I believe without it, the offering becomes a stench to God's nostrils instead of a sweet smell.

Strategies (Part II)

2 Timothy 4:1-8 – A Charge

Finally, my brothers and sisters I charge thee in the sight of God, and of Christ Jesus, who shall judge the living and the dead, and by his appearing and his kingdom: preach, teach, proclaim, the Word; be urgent in season, out of season; when you feel like it and when you don't; rebuke, exhort, with all longsuffering and teaching. A time is going to come when people will not endure sound doctrine; but, having itching ears, will heap to themselves teachers after their own lusts; and will turn away their ears from the truth, and turn aside unto fables. But be thou sober in all things, suffer hardship, do the work of an evangelist, fulfil thy ministry. For I am already being offered, and the time of my departure is come. I have fought the good fight, I have finished the course, I have kept the faith: henceforth there is laid up for me the crown of righteous- ness, which the Lord, the righteous judge, shall give to me at that day; and not to me only, but also to all them that have loved his appearing. (***AMP and authors interpretation***)

Thank you for allowing me this opportunity to take you to "boot camp" use this course as a refresher and as a new learning tool for teachers and Christian that need to tighten it up.

Final instructions: Forward march!

Answer Sheet

Work Page I (Personal)

Work Page II

Genesis	Isaiah	Romans
Exodus	Jeremiah	I Corinthians
Leviticus	Lamentations	2 Corinthians
Numbers	Ezekiel	Galatians
Deuteronomy	Daniel	Ephesians
Joshua	Hosea	Philippians
Judges	Joel	Colossians
Ruth	Amos	I Thessalonians
I Samuel	Obadiah	2 Thessalonians
2 Samuel	Jonah	I Timothy
I Kings	Micah	2 Timothy
2 Kings	Nahum	Titus
I Chronicles	Habakkuk	Philemon
2 Chronicles	Zephaniah	Hebrews
Ezra	Haggai	James
Nehemiah	Zechariah	I Peter
Esther	Malachi	2 Peter
Job	St. Matthew	I John
Psalms	St. Mark	2 John
Proverbs	St. Luke	3 John
Ecclesiastes	St. John	Jude
Song of Solomon	Acts	Revelation

Work Page III   Various Scriptures

Work Page IV   Various Scriptures

Work Page VII

1. Infirmity – I Cor. 12:9, Isa. 53:5
2. Rebellion – I Cor. 12:9-12, Matt. 19:18
3. Spirit of Error – I John 4:6; Psalms 51:10
4. Fear – 2 Tim. 1:7
5. Bondage – Rom. 8:15
6. Heaviness – Isa. 61:3
7. Haughtiness – Prov. 16:10, Rom. 1:4
8. Perverse spirit – Zech. 12:10, Heb. 10:29
9. Lying spirit – John 14:17, 15:26, 16:13
10. Jealousy – Eph. 5:2, I Cor. 13

Various Styles of Christian Music
(Please note these are just a few that I personally like in no specific order)

Praise is what I Do - Shekinah Glory
New Season - Israel and New Breed
If we Pray - Anointed
Adoration - Richard Smallwood
Around the Throne - Visions
Early Morning Worship - Thomas Michael
The Healing Starts Right There - Ted & Sheri
Bow Down and Worship Him - F.G.B.C.
Fellowship Mass Choir
The Minstrel - Ben Tankard
Tribe of Benjamin
Worship - Michael W. Smith
Psalms - Shane Barnard

To Contact Elder Rocheroyl Lowery, write:

Salah Ministries
P.O. Box 1382
Calumet City, IL. 60409
E-mail: salahministries@aol.com

Other books scheduled for release
Is it going to Hurt? Getting closer to the sacred
Up Close and Personal, The Anatomy of God,
The Inner Circle, Church Administration

Printed in the United States
6561